# GERBIL GENIUS

*Books in the Animal Ark Pets series*

Ben M. Baglio

# GERBIL GENIUS

Illustrated by
Paul Howard

Cover illustration by
Chris Chapman

A
**LITTLE APPLE**
PAPERBACK

SCHOLASTIC INC.
New York Toronto London Auckland Sydney

Special thanks to Pat Posner.
Thanks also to C.J. Hall, B.Vet.Med., M.R.C.V.S., for reviewing
the veterinary material contained in this book.

ISBN 0-590-59681-0

12 11 10 9 8 7 6 5 4 3 2 1                     8 9/9 0 1 2 3/0

Printed in the U.S.A.                               40
First Scholastic printing, March 1998

# Contents

# 1

# *Mouse Counting Day*

Mandy Hope was standing at her bedroom window listening to the church bells ringing out over Welford village. Her grandpa was one of the bell ringers and Mandy sometimes tried to guess which bell he was ringing.

But today, Mandy was waiting impatiently for the bells to stop. Then she could go and meet Grandpa, her best friend, James Hunter, and his dad, who lived at the other end of the village. The four of them had something very special to do this morning.

Mandy stuck her head further out of the window. The sun was shining, but there was a gentle breeze. She smiled as the wind ruffled her hair. Perfect weather.

Suddenly Mandy heard another sound — a fretful whining coming from the modern building attached to the back of the house. Mandy's parents were both vets at Animal Ark, and the extension was their clinic. The whining was coming from the unit, a special room where animals stayed if they weren't well enough to go home.

That's probably Sasha, Mandy told herself, pulling her head back inside the window. She decided to ask her mom if she could give the dog a quick cuddle.

Dr. Emily Hope was on her way to the clinic when Mandy bounded downstairs. "Can I go and see Sasha, Mom?" asked Mandy, as her mom opened the door that led from the house to the clinic.

"Okay. Just for a minute or two," Dr. Emily replied.

Sasha was an Afghan hound. She'd had a small lump removed from her eyelid. "She'll be going home today," said Dr. Emily. She smiled as she watched Mandy stroking the beautiful dog.

"What about Smudge?" asked Mandy, moving to another large cage where a young black and white cat was pacing restlessly. Smudge had been in a fight with another cat and he had seven stitches in his ear.

"He can go home, too," said Dr. Emily. "I'll call Naomi Bruce in a little while and tell her she can come and get him."

"That's good," said Mandy. "He doesn't like being shut up in this cage. Do you, boy?" Mandy rubbed his nose through the bars. Smudge glared at her and meowed loudly.

"Come on," said Dr. Emily. "We'll leave them to rest now."

They went back into the house and Mandy hurried to the kitchen and ran to the back door. "The bells have stopped," she said. "I can go and meet Grandpa now!"

"Why? Are you going somewhere with him?" asked Dr. Adam Hope as he came into the kitchen.

"Dad! You haven't really forgotten what's happening today, have you?" said Mandy.

"Stop teasing her, Adam," laughed Dr. Emily. "You know why Mandy's meeting Grandpa."

"And James and his dad," Mandy said happily.

Dr. Adam smiled and pointed to the calendar on the kitchen wall. Next to today's date Mandy had written the words **MOUSE COUNTING DAY** in big red letters. "I couldn't really forget what you're doing today, could I?" he chuckled. "Off you go, and good luck."

"Don't forget to take the mixed seed," said Dr. Emily, pointing to two brown paper bags on the kitchen table.

"Thanks, Mom." Mandy picked them up. "I'll see you both later," she said and hurried off.

The others were waiting for her outside the general store.

"I thought you were never going to get here, Mandy," said James when she raced up to them. "My dad and I have been here for ages."

"I went into the unit to see Sasha and Smudge," puffed Mandy as she hugged Grandpa. "It must have taken longer than I thought."

Mr. Hunter smiled. "Don't pay any attention to James, Mandy. We've only been here a couple of minutes. We arrived at the same time as your grandpa."

"Well, it seemed like ages to me," said James, pushing his glasses further on to the bridge of his nose.

They turned on to the narrow street at the side of the general store. This was a shortcut to the river. As they hurried along, they saw Mrs. Ponsonby walking toward them. She lived in Bleakfell Hall, a huge gray stone house on the outskirts of Welford. Mrs. Ponsonby often came to the village; she liked to keep an eye on what was happening there.

Mrs. Ponsonby was wearing a large straw hat with poppies around the brim and a white dress with a pattern of blue, red, yellow, and orange flowers all over it.

"She looks like a flower shop," James whispered to Mandy.

Mandy nodded and smiled. Mrs. Ponsonby always seemed to wear colorful clothes and big hats. Then Mandy noticed Pandora, Mrs. Ponsonby's plump Pekingese. Pandora was wearing a straw hat, too!

"The poor little darling gets so hot," said Mrs. Ponsonby when she saw Mandy looking at the hat. "She begged so hard to go for a walk along the riverbank that I put her sun hat on so she wouldn't get sunstroke."

"Good morning, Mr. Hope, Mr. Hunter," she added as Grandpa and James's dad got close. "You'll never guess what someone has done to the reed beds!"

Mrs. Ponsonby didn't wait for a reply. She continued indignantly, "Someone has dumped loads of old tennis balls there. It's a disgrace, that's what it is. I'm going to report it to the council first thing tomorrow and have them removed."

Mandy and James gazed at each other in dismay. Then Mandy blurted out, "You didn't *do* anything to the tennis balls, did you, Mrs. Ponsby? You see, *we* put the tennis balls there. I mean some of us from school put them there."

"They're special feeding houses," added James. "The balls have little holes in one side for a door and we slotted a bamboo cane through two slits on the back of each ball."

"Then we stuck the canes upright into the ground and put some mixed seed inside each mouse house," said Mandy. "And —"

"*Mouse* house?" interrupted Mrs. Ponsonby.

Mandy almost giggled. She thought Mrs. Ponsonby had sounded just like a mouse herself.

Then Grandpa explained that Mandy and James's school was taking part in a survey to find out how common harvest mice were in different areas all over the country.

"In some parts of the country, farmers grow more than one crop of hay or wheat a year," said James. "That means they're cutting the hay and wheat down just at the time the harvest mice want to build their nests. The survey will help us find out if the mice have found different places to live."

"We put fifty mouse houses in the reed beds

on Friday," said Mandy. "Today we're going to check how many have been used. It's our first mouse counting day!"

"You mean you're going to look inside each house and see if there's a mouse there?" shuddered Mrs. Ponsonby.

Mandy shook her head. "We're going to look inside and see if the seeds we put there have been eaten," she explained. "If they have, it will mean a harvest mouse has eaten them, because the little hole is too small for other creatures to use. Then we'll *know* there are harvest mice here. It will be great if we do find a mouse in a house," she added. "But I don't think we will."

"I still think the tennis balls are a bit of an eyesore," said Mrs. Ponsonby. "But," she added, giving a small bow, "seeing as you're carrying out a survey, I won't ask to have them removed."

"Whew!" breathed James as they watched Mrs. Ponsonby totter away on her high-heeled shoes. "Good thing we explained it all. It would have been awful if she'd done something to get our mouse houses taken away."

"Well, it's all settled now," said Grandpa. "Let's get a move on it and do some counting," he added, smiling down at his granddaughter.

A little while later, Mandy and James had worked their way along one row of mouse houses. Grandpa and Mr. Hunter were working their way along another row. "Eight of the houses along this row are empty," she said, beaming. "That means something has eaten the seed. Right, James?"

James nodded happily. "Yes," he said, popping some more seed through a small hole in one of the empty houses.

Mr. Hunter told them he and Mr. Hope had found five empty houses on their row.

"That means . . ." Mandy did a quick count, ". . . thirteen out of twenty-two mouse houses have been used."

"But," James worked a sum out in his head, "there are still twenty-eight mouse houses to check!"

"How can anyone really figure out how many harvest mice are here?" asked Mr. Hunter. "It might just be one eating all the seeds."

"That mouse would be a happy, *fat* one, Dad!" said James. Then he added, "Our teachers, Mrs. Black and Mrs. Todd, said we won't be able to figure *that* out correctly."

Mandy nodded. "They said that part of it will have to be guesswork. They said we should count three empty houses as one harvest mouse."

"But the main thing," James stated, "is that we know for sure that there *are* harvest mice here."

"Come on, then, let's start on the next row!" Mandy hurried over and bent down in front of a mouse house. The cane was quite tall, but the tennis ball house was only about nineteen inches from the ground.

Mandy carefully pulled the little house off its bamboo cane. She held it in one hand and shook it over the palm of her other. "No seed left in this one!" she said to James.

She replaced the tennis ball and walked a few steps to get some seed. The houses were about forty inches apart. She and James were sharing one bag of seed and Grandpa and Mr. Hunter were sharing the other. "We'll have to tell the others to bring a small bag of seed *each*," Mandy said. "It won't take us long then."

"Good idea," agreed James. "I don't need any for this house, though, there's still lots of seed in it." He put the house back and walked on, leaving the next mouse house he passed for Mandy to check.

Suddenly Grandpa appeared behind the mouse house Mandy was about to check. "I'm sure I heard a noise coming from inside this one," he whispered, bending down.

"You mean there's a mouse inside?" Mandy said excitedly.

Grandpa nodded. "I think there could be!" he said.

# 2

# *A Big Surprise*

Mandy knelt down to listen and her eyes
widened as she heard a strange little thumping
noise. It lasted for only a second, but she *knew*
she'd heard it. Maybe a harvest mouse was
building a nest inside the feeding house. Mrs.
Todd, her teacher, had said that might happen,

because the tennis balls were almost the same size and shape as a harvest mouse's nest.

Mandy signaled to James, then shuffled along on her knees, edging herself closer to the mouse house. She was trying really hard to move silently, but the tops of her shoes brushed some reeds and they rustled slightly. Mandy froze and glanced at James as the thumping noise from inside the mouse house started again.

"Wow!" breathed James, his eyes shining with excitement.

"If that's a harvest mouse it must be wearing shoes to make that sort of noise!" said Grandpa.

James and Mandy listened to the drumming noise and stared at the tennis ball mouse house. Then James pointed to the door hole. "See that, Mandy? The hole's been made bigger."

"The harvest mouse probably made it bigger so it could carry nesting material in," Mandy whispered. "Maybe the mouse is planning to cover the hole with leaves and grass from the inside. Oh, I wish we could peep in, but that might frighten it and make it run off."

"Let's just watch for a while," James suggested. "It might come out if it thinks we've gone. Then it would be safe to look in."

Mandy nodded. She hoped the harvest mouse *would* come out. She'd never seen a real live one close up. She'd never seen a harvest mouse's nest, either, other than in photos or on television. Now, she and James might see both. It would be great telling everyone at school about it tomorrow!

Grandpa and Mr. Hunter finished off the mouse house count on their own, while James and Mandy sat with their eyes glued to the door hole of the tennis ball.

After a while, they returned and crouched down beside Mandy and James.

Grandpa said quietly, "We've added all the figures up and, altogether, twenty-eight houses are being used."

"Over half. That's great!" Mandy exclaimed.

"I've written it down in the notebook for you, James," Mr. Hunter told him.

"Thanks, Dad," whispered James. "I think Mandy and I will stay here a while if that's okay."

"We want to know if the harvest mouse is nesting in there," said Mandy. "We'll come home as soon as we find out."

Another half an hour went by before anything happened. Then a face appeared at the door hole. It was a dark golden color and, for a moment, two big, round, dark eyes stared unblinkingly at Mandy and James. The creature's ears were standing straight up, its brown nose and long whiskers were twitching. Then the face disappeared.

Startled, Mandy and James gazed at each other. They'd only seen the creature for a second or two, but they both knew it definitely *wasn't* a harvest mouse!

"It's a gerbil!" Mandy whispered. "Oh, James, the poor little thing must have gotten out of its cage and made its way outside. Gerbils can't survive out of doors in this country, can they? We'll have to take it to Animal Ark."

James nodded. "But we'd better not try to get it out," he whispered back. "It might escape again. We'll have to carry it there in the mouse house, Mandy."

They got quietly to their feet and tiptoed closer to the tennis ball. They heard the gerbil give a frightened squeak, then they saw its face at the door hole again. As quick as a flash, James darted forward and put both hands around the tennis ball, covering the door hole with the palm of one hand.

"Good job," said Mandy with a relieved smile. "It would have been awful if it had gotten away!"

Keeping the ball clasped firmly between his hands, James straightened up and eased the ball off the cane. "Let's go," he said with a triumphant smile.

As they hurried off to Animal Ark, Mandy couldn't help wondering about the gerbil they had found. They had two pet gerbils in her class at school and Mrs. Todd had told them that gerbils burrowed. Mandy wondered why this gerbil had gone into the mouse house instead of tunneling and making itself a burrow.

"Maybe the soil was too hard or too crumbly for him to dig a burrow," she said aloud.

James nodded and glanced at the ball he was holding tightly in both hands. "I've been thinking about that," he said. "Maybe he did make a burrow somewhere. He might have come out and seen the harvest mice going into the houses and guessed there was food inside."

"He must have been really hungry," said Mandy. "Or . . ." She clapped her hand over her mouth.

"Or what?" James asked urgently.

"Maybe he's sick or hurt and went in the house to hide because he wasn't strong enough to make a burrow!" she said.

There wasn't far to go now. They were both worried that the gerbil might need help, so they walked as fast as they could.

# 3

# *A Worrying Time*

Dr. Emily was sitting on a lounge chair on the patio, reading the Sunday paper, when Mandy and James arrived at Animal Ark. Mandy flung open the back gate and ran across the lawn, leaving James to follow more slowly with the gerbil.

"Mom!" said Mandy, bounding up onto the patio.

Dr. Emily lowered her newspaper. "Is something wrong?" she asked, seeing Mandy's anxious expression.

Mandy nodded and pointed to James, who was walking toward them with the mouse house clasped firmly between his hands.

"Grandpa said you'd heard noises from inside one of the mouse houses," said Dr. Emily, getting to her feet. "Is it an injured harvest mouse?"

"It's a gerbil, Dr. Emily," said James, looking up with a worried expression.

Dr. Emily glanced doubtfully at the mouse house.

"We *both* saw his face, Mom," said Mandy. "We're really sure it's a gerbil."

"Okay. We'll go and have a look," said Dr. Emily.

"Oh, no," said Dr. Adam as they trooped through the kitchen. "I was just about to make ice-cream sodas. But something tells me this is another animal rescue."

"Could be," Dr. Emily replied. "Mandy and James think there's a gerbil in this mouse house."

As the three of them went into the clinic, Dr. Emily asked Mandy to get a cardboard pet carrier.

James followed Dr. Emily into the treatment room. She put on her white vet's coat, then smiled at James as he rested his cupped hands on the examination table. "I bet your fingers are aching," she said.

James nodded. "I've been keeping them tightly over the door hole in case the gerbil jumps out and gets away," he said. "We heard him squeaking before, but he didn't make any noise all the way here. Do you think he might be sick, Dr. Emily?"

"We'll soon find out, James," Dr. Emily replied as she pulled on a pair of rubber gloves.

Mandy came in with the pet carrier and put it on the table with a puzzled look. She didn't know why her mom wanted such a large box for a gerbil.

When Dr. Emily opened up the carrier she put an empty metal instrument tray in and told James to lower the mouse house to the bottom of the carrier. Then she put her hand over James's. "Okay," she said quietly. "Move your hands away now, James."

James slowly moved his hand from under Dr. Emily's. Then he sighed with relief and wriggled his fingers. But he didn't take his eyes off the mouse house.

"What are you going to do, Mom?" asked Mandy.

"I'm going to tip him into a corner and use the tray as a barrier," Dr. Emily explained. "In case whatever it is tries to jump."

Mandy and James held their breath as Dr. Emily lifted the tennis ball ever so slightly, tilting it so the door hole was facing toward one corner of the carrier.

A small, browny-gold animal slid out, head first. It quickly rose up on its hind legs, curling its smaller front legs and little clawed feet inward under its neck, showing the paler color of its chest and tummy. Although it was the same shape as a mouse, it was a bit bigger.

"It *is* a gerbil!" said Dr. Emily. "I really thought you two had made a mistake," she admitted. "I was expecting a giant harvest mouse to pop out of the mouse house."

For a second the gerbil seemed to be frozen to the spot. Mandy bit her lip. The poor little thing was so scared — its dark chocolate-brown eyes were huge with fright.

Dr. Emily put the ball down gently and very slowly tilted the metal tray. The gerbil lowered its front legs and then, with small, alarmed squeaks, it darted into the corner. It pressed its pointed snout right against the cardboard.

They could see its body trembling and its tail — about the same length as its body — lay straight out behind it, resting on the bottom of the carrier.

The lower half of the gerbil's tail looked really strange — as if the fur had been shaved

off. It was pink and sore-looking, too! Mandy pointed and lifted worried eyes to her mom's face.

Dr. Emily nodded, straightened up, and closed the carrier. "The skin covering his tail has been shed," she explained. "That *can* happen if gerbils are picked up by the end of their tails. In this case a cat might have clawed at his tail and damaged it."

"Poor gerbil," Mandy sighed. "What happens next, Mom?"

"Well, first, I'll put him into a cage and allow him to calm down for a while," Dr. Emily replied.

"Will you be able to make his tail better, Dr. Emily?" asked James.

Dr. Emily looked from one worried face to the other. "I'm afraid I'll have to remove most of it," she said gently. "The skin won't grow back. If we leave it like that, the sore part will become infected and make him ill."

Mandy blinked hard and James took off his glasses and wiped them on his T-shirt.

"He should be all right afterward," Dr. Emily continued. "He just won't be able to balance so well when he's sitting up or jumping."

"But you really think he'll be okay, Mom?"

"I'll need to take a closer look at him, Mandy. But from what I have seen he appears to be healthy enough. His coat is sleek and in good condition and there aren't any sore spots around his eyes, ears, or nose. Either he hasn't been living wild for long, or he's managed to find the right sort of food to keep him healthy."

"His coat is sleek, isn't it?" said Mandy, looking a bit happier.

"And his eyes are very bright," said James. "But that might be because he's still frightened."

Dr. Emily nodded and explained that gerbils were often nervous when being handled by someone they didn't know.

"Or," Mandy said thoughtfully, "if he's been living wild for a while, he could have forgotten about a human being a friend."

"Yes, that's possible," Dr. Emily agreed. "Now," she added, picking up the carrier, "I'll go and find him a cage and leave him in the unit for a while."

Mandy and James went back into the kitchen where Mandy told her dad all about the gerbil.

"I wonder where he escaped from?" said Dr. Adam. "I haven't heard anything about a lost gerbil."

"We need a name for him," said James. "Why don't we take Blackie for a walk later and try to think of one?"

"That's an excellent idea, James," said Dr. Adam, smiling down at Mandy's friend.

Mandy managed a smile, too. She was still worried about the gerbil, but it would be great thinking of a name for him. And it would be fun taking Blackie for a walk. Blackie was James's Labrador puppy. He hadn't learned to do as he was told yet, but Mandy really loved Blackie.

"I'll come by right after lunch," said Mandy. "And we could drop in at Lilac Cottage afterwards and tell Grandma and Grandpa about the gerbil."

"Lunch!" gasped James in dismay. "I'm going to be really late. I'd better get going."

Mandy watched James run off and then went into the kitchen to get ready for lunch. She kept glancing toward the door, though, impatient for her mom to tell her more about the gerbil.

# 4

# *Name Problem*

"He's probably about five or six months old," said Dr. Emily when she came into the kitchen. "I picked him up to put him in the cage and his weight is fine. Apart from his tail, there doesn't seem to be anything wrong with him."

"It's too bad about his tail," Mandy sighed. "I hope he knows you'll only be doing it to help him."

Dr. Emily gave her a quick hug. "I had a little chat with him and explained what I was going to do and why I had to do it," she replied. "He squeaked at me and I think he was telling me 'Okay.'"

Mandy giggled. Her mom knew just how to cheer her up.

While she was eating her lunch, Mandy's mind buzzed with possible names for the gerbil. Sandy . . . Goldie . . . Woffles . . . No! That sounded like a name for a rabbit. Jimmy . . . Lucky . . . Squeaker . . .

Mandy shook her head. None of them sounded right. She'd have to wait and see if James had any better ideas.

When Mandy got close to James's house she could see Blackie's nose poking out through the bars in the front gate. She laughed out loud and Blackie gave a joyful woof. Then he leaped up at the gate, scrabbling his front paws crazily along the top of it.

"He's been watching for you," said James, running to get hold of Blackie's collar. "I told him we'd be going for a walk when you got here. I'm sure he understood."

"Of course he did," said Mandy, opening the gate and slipping through. "He's a smart boy; aren't you, Blackie?"

Blackie's tail wagged furiously and he lowered his head to Mandy's feet. "No, Blackie," Mandy chuckled. "There aren't any laces for you to pull at!"

The Labrador loved pulling at shoelaces, but this afternoon Mandy was wearing flip-flops. Blackie soon found something else to do. He started sniffing and licking at Mandy's bare toes. "Ooh!" she laughed. "That tickles. Stop it, Blackie!"

James pulled Blackie away and clipped his leash on. "Now calm down and walk nicely," he said sternly, opening the gate.

As they walked toward the park, Mandy told
her friend what her mom had said. Then she
sighed and added, "I guess she'll be operating
on his tail tomorrow, after he's settled."

"It's too bad about his tail," said James. "But
it's lucky we found him before it got any worse."

"Lucky is one of the names I thought of
while I was eating my lunch," said Mandy.

James wrinkled his nose and shook his head.
He didn't think Lucky sounded right, either.
They walked on in silence for a while, both

trying to think of a good name. By the time they reached the park neither of them had thought of one.

"There's Arnie," said Mandy, "sitting next to the bench by the tennis courts."

"Guarding Mr. Jordan's bag while he plays tennis," said James.

Mike Jordan was about Grandpa Hope's age. He hadn't lived in Welford long, but he got to know people because of Arnie.

Everyone loved Arnie. He was a comical-looking dog who was always getting into places he couldn't get himself out of. He was dark brown, tan, and white — a cross between a dachshund and a Boston terrier. His body was long and he had a very broad, muscular chest. His front legs curved outward slightly and seemed too long for his body. His tail was long and curled over. He had a really cute face and big ears that stood straight up.

"We'll have to tell Arnie how we rescued the gerbil," James joked as they wandered over to him.

Mandy smiled. Arnie was *always* rescuing things. Hedgehogs, baby birds, kittens — if any small creature was where Arnie thought it shouldn't be, he'd pick it up gently in his mouth and take it home. Then, Mr. Jordan would have to try to find out where the animal had come from.

"Arnie's name really fits him," Mandy said as she bent down to stroke him. "I wish we could think of a good name for our gerbil."

"*Our* gerbil?" asked James, smiling as Blackie and Arnie greeted each other.

"Well, he's ours for the time being," said Mandy, waving to Mr. Jordan as he came to pick up a tennis ball from the back of the court.

Mandy knew that if nobody claimed the gerbil they'd have to find him a good home. The Hopes were too busy looking after other people's animals for them to have a pet of their own.

"I'm going to ask Mom and Dad if we can take care of him," said Mandy. "It would be great, because gerbils are awake in the day. I want to do *everything* for him: feed him, clean his cage, play with him . . ." She paused and bit her lip. "He'll have to get used to us before we can play with him. We'll have to talk to him a lot, then he'll come to us when we call him."

"Yup." James frowned. "So he really does need a name. Let's start walking again, Mandy. I can think better then."

They said good-bye to Arnie. He didn't seem to mind them going, and he soon went back to guarding his master's bag.

Mandy noticed a small crowd standing and sitting around the bandstand. "There must be a brass band concert today," she said.

James nodded. "The local band plays here most Sundays. We can hear it from our garden."

"I wonder if Pam Stanton's here," said Mandy. "Her dad plays the trombone."

Pam was in Mandy's class at school. She had a guinea pig named Ginny, and Mandy and James knew she'd want to hear about the gerbil.

"She is," James pointed. "See, Mandy, she's over there."

"So are Grandma and Grandpa!" said Mandy, starting to run.

"Hi," said Pam, when they ran up to her. "Did you get to see the harvest mouse? Your grandpa's just been telling me you heard one inside a mouse house." She bent down to stroke Blackie.

Mandy and James told Pam, Grandma, and Grandpa about the gerbil.

"Good heavens," said Grandma, shaking her head. "Who would have thought it? That's one very bright gerbil."

"It's fantastic!" said Pam. "I wish I'd been there. You'll have to pin a notice on the school bulletin board tomorrow telling everyone you've found a gerbil. Just think," she continued, "if it hadn't been for our harvest mouse survey — "

"That's it!" James interrupted. "Mandy, I've just thought of a perfect name for him."

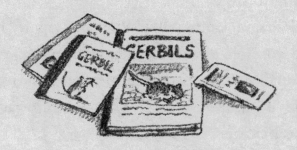

# 5

# *Harvey*

"Harvey!" James said, beaming triumphantly. "Because we found him in a harvest mouse's house!"

"Harvey," repeated Mandy. "Yes! It's absolutely perfect!"

Pam looked at them and burst out laughing.

"What's wrong? Don't you like it, Pam?" asked Mandy, feeling disappointed.

"It's not that! It's just that . . ." Pam laughed again, ". . . whenever my dad sees Ginny he wiggles his nose at her and my mom says he looks more like a *gerbil* than a guinea pig," she chortled, glancing toward the bandstand where the band members were busy setting everything up. "And Dad's name is Harvey!"

Mandy and James looked toward Mr. Stanton. He was holding his trombone to his mouth and Mandy giggled. "Wouldn't our Harvey look funny playing a trombone?" she said.

Grandma laughed, too, then she held a finger to her mouth; the concert was about to begin.

The music was soft and slow at first, but gradually it got louder and faster. Blackie sat down. His ears pricked up. He held his head first to one side, then to the other, then . . . he pointed his head to the sky and started howling!

"Oh, no!" said James, frantically tugging at

Blackie's collar. "Let's get away from here, Mandy!" But Blackie didn't want to move. James's face grew redder and redder as he tried to get Blackie to stand up.

In the end, Grandpa bent down and lifted Blackie's bottom from the ground. Then he dug in his pocket and passed a couple of bills to Mandy. "Go and buy some ice cream," he said, his mouth close to Blackie's ears.

*Ice cream!* Blackie seemed to recognize that. He looked up at James and then tugged at his leash.

"Thanks, Mr. Hope," James called over his shoulder as he and Mandy hurried off with Blackie leading the way.

Mandy bought two ice creams from the truck. Blackie started to whine when he saw them and looked pleadingly at James. "You don't deserve any," James told him. "But . . ." James pulled a doggy treat out of his pocket and put the *tiniest* bit of ice cream on it. "Just to let him think he's got one of his own," he said to Mandy.

Mandy nodded. They knew dogs shouldn't have ice cream, but the speck James had given him wouldn't do any harm.

"Let's go back to Animal Ark," said Mandy when they'd finished eating. "I can't wait to ask Mom and Dad if we can look after Harvey."

Dr. Emily was sitting at the big pine table doing some paperwork when Mandy, James, and Blackie burst into the kitchen.

"We've thought of a perfect name for the gerbil, Mom!" said Mandy.

Mandy's mom agreed that Harvey was a good name, then she looked closely at Mandy's face. "I recognize that expression, Mandy Hope," she said. "What else have you thought of?"

Mandy rubbed one foot against the ankle of her other foot. "I know we won't be able to *keep* Harvey, Mom, but please could James and I look after him while he is here?"

"We mean clean out his cage and everything, Dr. Emily," said James, shoving his glasses back on to the bridge of his nose.

Mandy said they knew it would mean a lot of hard work and they'd have to be very patient with Harvey. "He'll be frightened of us for a while, so we'll have to talk to him a lot so he gets to know us and trust us. And I know we'd have to *learn* exactly how to look after him, Mom. But we'd read about that, wouldn't we, James?"

Dr. Adam's deep laugh sounded from the doorway. He had a couple of slim books and some pamphlets in one hand. He held them up and waved them at Mandy and James. Blackie woofed and darted over to say hello. He was very fond of Mandy's dad.

"Whoa there, young fella! These aren't for you," said Dr. Adam as Blackie leaped up, trying to reach the books. "They're for Mandy and James."

"For us, Dad?" Mandy hurried to take them from him.

"From the clinic," he told her.

Mandy glanced down at them, then she flung her arms around her dad's waist. "How did you know?" she said. "How did you know what we were talking about?"

"Magic," he teased, ruffling her hair. Blackie gave another woof and jumped up again.

"Both of you at once is too much!" Dr. Adam protested.

Mandy moved away and thrust the books and pamphlets into her friend's hands with a huge smile. They were all about caring for gerbils; feeding them, taming them, keeping them healthy . . .

"Wow!" said James, grinning back at Mandy.

Dr. Emily smiled. "We guessed you would ask if you could look after him," she said. "But," she added, "you'll have to wait until he starts recovering."

"That'll give us time to read the books and pamphlets, right, James?"

"From cover to cover," he said.

"I put a notice on the clinic bulletin board asking if anyone has lost a gerbil," said Dr. Adam.

"And we'll put one on the school bulletin board," said James.

"That's a good idea," Dr. Adam said. "But if nobody's claimed him in a week or so . . ." he looked meaningfully at Mandy, ". . . we'll have to start looking for a good home for him."

Mandy met his gaze and nodded. She didn't like thinking about that, but at least they'd have Harvey for a little while.

James had wandered to the kitchen table and was sitting with his head propped in his hands — he was reading one of the pamphlets already. Mandy dragged a chair around so she

could sit next to him. She reached out for one of the books and opened it.

A few seconds later her mom said, "I thought I'd have the kitchen to myself for a while to do my paperwork, and now there are two eager beavers at the table and one pest of a dog chewing at my laces!"

James jumped up looking really worried. Mandy giggled and pulled him back down. She knew her mom was teasing. "We want to make sure we know everything there is to know, Mom. While Harvey's here, he'll be the best-looked-after gerbil ever!" she said.

# 6

# *Spreading the News*

Next morning there was no sign of James when Mandy arrived at the huge, old oak tree on the village green. They always met there to bike the rest of the way to school together.

Mandy propped her bike against the tree and went over to the pond to look at the tadpoles. She knelt down and peered into the water.

The tadpoles were getting really big now; some of them had grown two tiny back legs. Mandy knew their front legs were growing as well, but they were hidden by little gill plates. When the gills disappeared she'd be able to see the front legs, too. And, soon after, the tadpoles' tails would get shorter and shorter . . . "Then," Mandy murmured, "you'll change into little frogs and be hopping all over the green!"

Mandy watched for a little while longer until she heard someone calling her name. She stood up and turned to see Paul Stevens propping his bike next to hers. Paul was eight and a year younger. He was in the same class as James. He lived in Jasmine Cottage near Grandma and Grandpa.

"Hi, Paul," said Mandy, walking to meet him. "How's Paddy?" Paddy was Paul's Exmoor pony.

"Fantastic," beamed Paul. "We went for a great ride over the moors with the pony club yesterday. How's the gerbil? Your grandpa told me about him last night. Did you really find him in one of our mouse houses?"

Mandy nodded, then told Paul the whole story. "I couldn't see him this morning. He's having his operation at nine o'clock and Mom didn't want him disturbed before."

"He'll probably be wide awake and running around when you get home from school," said Paul.

"I hope so," said Mandy. "Then tomorrow or the next day, James and I can start looking after him," she finished off happily.

"Let me know if you want any help," said Paul. "You and James were a big help when I first got Paddy from the rescue shelter."

Mandy explained that because Harvey had been living wild he'd probably be nervous around humans for a while.

Paul nodded. "Do you think I could come and see him when he isn't frightened of people anymore?"

"Of course you can, Paul," replied Mandy.

The church clock chimed in the distance and Mandy sighed. "I don't know where James is, but we'd better go or we'll be late."

Welford Village School was on Church Street — a small road off Main Street at the side of the church.

James caught up with Paul and Mandy just as they were biking past the church. He was pedaling furiously and looked hot and out of breath.

"Mom says Harvey's doing fine," Mandy told him. "Why are you so late, James? Did you oversleep?"

"I forgot the mouse count notebook," he replied breathlessly. "I had to go back for it."

The notebook was important. They were supposed to take it to Mrs. Garvie, the principal, before the school assembly. Mrs. Garvie was going to tell the whole school the results of the first mouse counting day.

"I almost forgot the notice for the bulletin board," Mandy admitted as they rode toward the bike rack. She and James had written it yesterday before James had gone home.

When they'd wheeled their bikes into the special racks, Mandy opened her schoolbag and pulled the notice out to show Paul. It had a drawing of a mouse house in the middle, and around the drawing were the words:

*Mandy Hope and James Hunter found a gerbil in a mouse house.*

*We are calling him Harvey.*

*If anyone has lost a gerbil please contact Animal Ark.*

"What will happen if you don't find his owner?" Paul asked. "He probably doesn't belong to anyone from school because someone would have put a notice on the board about a lost gerbil."

Mandy told him her dad put a notice up on Animal Ark's board, too.

"But if nobody claims him, we'll have to find him a good home," said James. Then he looked up at the school building and saw Mrs. Garvie looking down at them from her office window. "We'd better hurry, Mandy. I think Mrs. Garvie is waiting for the notebook."

Paul said he'd put the notice up for them.

"Put it in the best place you can," Mandy called as she and James ran off.

"I see you found twenty-eight mouse houses with the food gone?" Mrs. Garvie said a short while later, as she looked at the mouse counting notebook.

Mandy and James nodded.

"And we decided to count one harvest mouse for every three empty mouse houses. So, how many harvest mice can we say are living in or around the reed beds?"

"At least nine, Mrs. Garvie," said Mandy.

The principal nodded and smiled. "I'll give out these details right after assembly. Then I'll send a report to all the other schools taking part in the survey. And I should be hearing from them soon with details of their first mouse counts."

Mandy and James looked at each other. Should they tell Mrs. Garvie about Harvey? She might not see the bulletin board until *after* she'd sent her report to all the other schools and they might be interested to know what they'd found in one of the mouse houses.

"Is there something else?" Mrs. Garvie asked.

Then Mandy and James told her all about it — from when Grandpa had heard something inside the mouse house, right up to why they'd decided to call the gerbil Harvey.

"Goodness," said Mrs. Garvie. "I think I'll have to make a special announcement about this after the mouse count report. Or better still, how about you two coming up on the platform and telling everyone yourselves?"

"We made a notice for the bulletin board and Paul Stevens is putting it up for us right now," James said in alarm. He didn't like the idea of standing up in front of the whole school!

"But we didn't tell the whole story," said Mandy. "I'll do the talking, James, if you want."

Mandy crossed her fingers while she waited for James's reply. She didn't *really* want to go up onto the platform on her own.

"No . . . it's okay, I'll do it with you," James said.

Mandy smiled happily at Mrs. Garvie. She knew James wouldn't let her down.

When the time came during assembly for Mandy and James to go up onto the platform, James felt nervous all over again. But once Mandy had started talking, he joined in eagerly. He even asked if anyone had lost a gerbil.

But nobody had lost a gerbil and everybody wondered where Harvey had lived before he found his way into one of their mouse houses.

Then Pam Stanton waved her hand in the air. She asked Mrs. Garvie if the school could have a Harvey announcement every day. "He *was* found in one of *our* mouse houses," she pointed out.

Mrs. Garvie thought every day would be a bit too much, but she said James and Mandy could give the school an update once a week.

"And," said Mandy to James at the end of the assembly, "we should have plenty to tell everyone next week. By then we'll have spent four or five days looking after Harvey. Oh," she added, hugging herself with excitement, "I just can't wait for Mom to tell us we can start!"

# 7

# *Making Friends*

After school, James and Mandy rode quickly to Animal Ark. Maybe they'd be able to see Harvey for a few minutes!

"That's if he's all right," said Mandy. She'd been worrying all day.

"I'm sure he will be," said James.

"I wonder if he'll be able to eat yet?" said

Mandy as they wheeled their bikes up the garden path. "If we knew his favorite food, we could put some in his cage to show him we're friends."

"What treats do Terry and Gerry like best?" James asked. Terry and Gerry were Mandy's class gerbils. Mandy and the rest of her class all helped look after them.

"Terry likes raisins and Gerry *loves* tomato," Mandy replied.

"Well, Harvey might like both of those," said James. "Let's ask your mom if it would be all right to give him some of each."

"Good idea," said Mandy. "Let's go and find her."

Dr. Emily was walking out of the unit when Mandy and James hurried into the clinic. "Harvey's fine," she said before Mandy had time to ask.

Mandy ran to hug her. "I knew he *would* be okay, Mom," she said. "But I couldn't help worrying."

"You can have five minutes with him," said

Dr. Emily. Her green eyes twinkled when she saw their excited faces.

Then Mandy's words tumbled out quickly as she told her mom what she and James had thought of. ". . . So do you think it would be all right to give Harvey a couple of raisins and a small piece of tomato?"

"I think it's a very good idea," said Dr. Emily. "But remember to move your hands very slowly when you're putting anything in the cage."

"So we don't frighten him," said James.

"That's right," said Dr. Emily. "And it's a little too soon to try to get him to take anything from your fingers. I think you'd better just put his treats near his food dish."

"I hope Harvey will like them," said Mandy.

"Me, too." Her mom smiled. "It might stop him from chewing the wood chips off the floor of his cage and throwing bits out through the bars!"

"Is that what he's been doing?" Mandy asked.

Dr. Emily nodded. "I think Harvey might be feeling a little bored. I've put a couple of cardboard tubes in his cage, but I think he needs something more interesting to play with," she told them. "I'm sure I can leave that to you two, though."

"You bet!" said James, edging to one side and trying to peer into the unit.

"Go ahead," Dr. Emily laughed. "You can look at Harvey while I get his treats."

Mandy followed James into the unit and over to Harvey's cage. There was no sign of the gerbil. Mandy thought he must be in his wooden nesting box at the back of the cage, but suddenly James pointed to one of the cardboard tubes.

The lower half of Harvey's face was peeping out of one end. His whiskers were twitching and he was staring at them, his eyes round and dark and curious.

"Let's crouch down and put our faces close to the cage," Mandy suggested quietly.

James nodded and, moving together, they slowly and silently bent down.

A little scratchy sound came from the tube — Harvey's claws moving inside. For a moment it seemed as though he was going to wriggle backward and hide away. Mandy and James froze, hardly daring to breathe. But Harvey stayed where he was.

"I think it would be all right for us to talk around him," Mandy whispered. "Get him used to the sound of our voices." Just then Harvey's front feet crept a little way out of the tube. The rest of his face began to appear and Mandy smiled as his ears, which must have been flattened against the inside of the tube, suddenly popped up.

"Hello, Harvey," Mandy said softly. "We won't hurt you. We want to be your friends."

James told Harvey he was a very brave gerbil.

Harvey stared solemnly back. Mandy was sure he was waiting for one of them to speak again.

Just then the unit door opened. Harvey scrabbled his feet, gave a frightened squeak, and, quick as a flash, withdrew his head and moved right back inside the tube.

Mandy and James stood up, and Simon, who'd recently come to work at Animal Ark, walked toward them. He was holding a plate containing a piece of tomato and two raisins. Simon wasn't a vet, he was a nurse. He helped with operations and looked after animals who had to stay for a while. He kept the animals clean and comfortable, soothed them and talked to them, changed dressings, fed them, and gave them any medicine they needed.

Mandy and James liked Simon. He was always willing to answer their questions and he knew a lot about animals.

"Your mom's been called out," Simon told Mandy. "She asked me to bring this in for you to give to the gerbil. And she said to remind you not to stay in here too long."

"We'll put Harvey's treats in the cage, then watch for a very *little* while to see if he comes out," said Mandy. "Will you wait with us, Simon?"

"Sure," he said. "But that doesn't mean you spend any more time with Harvey!"

Mandy smiled, then passed James the piece of tomato. He put it carefully into the cage. Mandy put the raisins next to it.

The three of them stepped back and waited. But not even a whisker appeared from the tube. "Come on," said Simon. "He'll probably pop out and gobble everything up as soon as we've gone."

"He let us look at him and talk to him for a while, Simon," Mandy said as she closed the unit door behind them. "But he didn't come out of the tube all the way, so we couldn't see his tail end."

"He's still got a bit of a tail," Simon told her. "About this much," he added, holding his thumb and forefinger about an inch apart.

"Maybe he'll let us see *all* of him next time," said James.

Simon nodded. "Gerbils are curious and

nosy little creatures," he said. "In time, wanting to know and see what's going on makes them forget their fear."

"Dr. Emily said he needs something interesting to play with," said James. "If we could think of something to put in his cage tomorrow, do you think he'd feel curious enough to go and look at it?"

Simon thought it was a good idea. Now all Mandy and James needed to do was to figure out something really interesting and exciting to make for Harvey.

"Call your mom and ask if you can stay for dinner, James," Mandy suggested. She knew her parents wouldn't mind; James was always welcome at Animal Ark.

"Okay," James agreed. "Then we can really think about it."

"Remember how we made an adventure playground for Frisky?" said James as he and Mandy set the table. "Well, maybe we could do something like that for Harvey."

Frisky was a small Russian hamster who had stayed with Mandy's grandparents while his owner was on vacation. Mandy and James had helped look after him for the whole week and they'd made his cage a really exciting play place for him.

"I read in one of those books Dad gave us that gerbils tend to be even more adventurous than hamsters," said Mandy. "We'll have to think of all sorts of things he can wiggle into and climb up. Maybe we could make him a maze out of little cardboard boxes with holes in the tops."

"We could leave one or two boxes open and put a little ladder or a thick branch in so he'll be able to climb up and down and in and out of them," said James.

"Sounds like gerbil talk to me," said a voice from the doorway.

It was Dr. Adam. He came in and put a narrow box with rounded ends on the table. "Nuts and raisins for you," he told Mandy. "Mrs. Edwards sent them. I was just there to check Tilly's puppies."

Mrs. Edwards had a grocery shop and Tilly was her corgi.

"How many puppies did she have, Dad? Are they okay?"

Dr. Adam smiled. "She had two; Mom and pups are doing fine. The puppies are both boys and they look just like their dad."

"Isn't their dad a corgi, too?" Mandy asked.

"No!" Dr. Adam's eyes twinkled. "Their dad is Mike Jordan's Arnie."

Mandy laughed. "We'd better not tell Arnie about his sons. He'll want to take them home and put them in his basket."

James didn't say a word. Mandy wondered why and turned to look at him. James was staring hard at the box of nuts and raisins. "You can have some if you want," Mandy told him.

Her friend shook his head. "It's not them, it's the box they're in," he explained. "I've thought of just the right thing to make for Harvey."

# 8

# *Gerbil Jinks*

Mandy was so curious about James's idea she couldn't eat her dinner fast enough. She finished long before her friend did and then had to wait for him!

She kept looking at the box, but she just couldn't guess what James had in mind.

But James finished at last and Mandy jumped

up to clear the table. Then she took the lid off the box and tipped the nuts and raisins into a small bowl. James reached for a nut and nibbled it as he gazed thoughtfully at the box.

"We need a small square or oblong box that will fit inside this one at one end," he said. "And some smaller boxes, too . . . and the inside of a paper towel roll to cut down for a funnel and —"

"I get it!" Mandy interrupted excitedly. "We're going to turn the box into a boat!"

"Yes!" James grinned up at her. "A cargo boat!"

"And the cargo will be food," said Mandy. "We've got some of the cargo already. We can hide some of the raisins or pieces of carrot or turnip or a grape inside the little boxes. Oh, it's a great idea, James! I'm sure there are cardboard tubes and little boxes in the clinic."

The cargo boat soon took shape. James carefully cut two holes in the box they were using for the bridge area, one hole for a door and the other to push the funnel into. Mandy cut holes in the smaller boxes and arranged them at the other end of the boat in a sort of maze.

"If Harvey likes his cargo boat, we can keep adding things to it," Mandy said happily.

"Mmm," James nodded. "A ladder would be good, wouldn't it? We could stand the boat on a block of wood or another box, so he'd have to climb up the ladder to get on to it."

Mandy decided a box would be better than a block of wood. "Because then," she said, "we can make *another* play area inside the box, and it will be —"

"A multistory play area!" James finished the sentence for her. "Wow!" he added. "I can't wait for tomorrow."

At school next day, Mrs. Garvie read the reports from some of the other schools taking part in the harvest mouse survey. One school said that none of the food had gone from the tennis ball mouse houses, and two other schools reported quite a high success rate.

"But nobody else found a gerbil in a mouse house!" said Carrie Anderson, who was in Mandy's class. "I've got something for Harvey," she said, and she handed Mandy a small wooden ball. "I bought it for Bingo, my bird," Carrie told her. "He doesn't play with it, so I thought Harvey might like it."

"That's great, Carrie. Thanks," said Mandy. When Mandy went to find James at play-time, he showed her a wooden brick with two holes in it.

"I brought it for Harvey," said Amy Fenton. "It's one especially for pets. Someone bought it for Minnie, but she's already got lots of play-things." Minnie was Amy's white mouse.

Mandy smiled. "Tell Minnie thank you," she said, then she showed James and Amy the little wooden ball Carrie had given her.

It wasn't Mandy's turn to feed Terry and Gerry, the class gerbils, but she watched Richard Tanner and Jill Redfern while they did it. She wanted to see what the gerbils liked best after raisins and tomato.

"I always bring Terry a small piece of parsley when it's my turn to feed him," said Jill.

"And Gerry likes sunflower seeds," said Richard, laughing as the gerbil scurried over and climbed into his hand to nibble the seed.

Mandy couldn't wait for the day when Harvey would be tame enough to do that!

"I know we've got to be patient," she said to James as they rode home from school. "But it'll be so nice when Harvey starts to trust us!"

When they hurried into the clinic, Dr. Adam greeted them with a smile. "I'm sure Harvey is waiting for you," he said. "He's had his nose pressed to the cage bars for the last ten minutes."

"Does he look all right?" Mandy asked. She felt a little bit worried about seeing him with just a tiny tail.

"He looks great," Dr. Adam assured her.

As soon as they went into the unit, Harvey started squeaking. Mandy beamed at James and they walked slowly toward the cage, talking in low voices.

They got closer and closer to the cage. Harvey squeaked again and then he rose up on his hind legs and gripped the cage bars with his front claws.

"This is a nice welcome," said Mandy, crouching down slowly. "And Dad's right. He looks great, James. His tiny tail doesn't make him look strange at all."

"He's got such a cute face, you don't really notice his tail's shorter than it should be," said James.

Harvey hadn't moved away from the cage bars, so James crouched down, too. "Hello, Harvey," he said. "We've made you something to play with. We'll go and get it in a minute. We'll bring you some treats to nibble, too. Then we'll feed you and give you some fresh water."

Harvey moved his head to one side and stared at James.

"I think he's starting to like us talking to him," Mandy said, and Harvey turned his head slightly and looked at her.

Then, very, very slowly, Mandy walked her fingers up the cage bars until they were close to Harvey's front paws. The gerbil pulled his body back a little way when she ran the tip of one finger over his curled claws, but he didn't take his paw away.

"See if he'll let you stroke his tummy, Mandy," said James.

"Okay," breathed Mandy, slowly moving her fingers down the bars.

Mandy stroked the soft, pale gold fur four times before Harvey decided he'd been brave enough! He moved away quickly with a little squeak and disappeared inside a cardboard tube.

Feeling happy and excited, Mandy and James went to find Dr. Adam to tell him the good news.

"That's really good progress," he said, smiling at them.

Mandy nodded. "And now we're going to get his cargo boat and some little treats to hide in the boxes. Do you think it would be all right to give him some sunflower seeds, Dad?"

"Just one or two," he said, going on to explain that too many sunflower seeds could cause skin problems for a gerbil.

Mandy said they'd hide only one sunflower seed to be on the safe side.

When they went into the kitchen, Dr. Emily was preparing dinner. "It's salad," she said. "I'm making it now so it will be ready to eat as soon as the clinic hours are over."

Mandy and James then told her all about Harvey, too, and they showed her the wooden ball and the brick with holes in it.

"That was nice of Carrie and Amy," said Dr. Emily. "But you'd better wash them in mild disinfectant and let them dry before you give them to Harvey, just to make sure there aren't any germs on them."

"We'll do that after we've given him this," said Mandy, reaching for the cargo boat she'd tucked away in a safe corner. "He can have them tomorrow."

James was watching Dr. Emily grate some cheese. She smiled and handed him a piece.

"Gerbils like cheese, don't they?" Mandy said. "I read it in one of the pamphlets."

"Yes, you can cut a small piece for him," her mom said.

"So we'll hide cheese, a sunflower seed, and . . . and what else, James?"

"Carrot?" said James, pointing to the bowl of salad.

"There'll be nothing left for us to eat at this rate," Dr. Emily teased as she lifted a small teaspoonful of grated carrot from the bowl.

When they'd hidden the food in three of the boxes in the little maze, they hurried through to the clinic and into the unit.

James opened Harvey's cage and carefully slid the cargo boat in. "Look, Mandy, he's watching from inside the tube," he said.

And almost before James had closed the cage door, Harvey was scampering eagerly toward his new boat. He ran all around the outside of it, sniffing and squeaking to himself. Then he climbed inside and went through the round door of the box that had the paper-towel-roll funnel sticking up through its top.

They could hear him moving around, then Mandy gave a little gasp and pointed to the funnel. It was slowly rising upward.

"He must be pushing the end that's inside the box with his head!" said James. "Isn't he smart? He's making up a game of his own!"

Harvey pushed the paper towel roll all the way out and the next minute he popped up through the hole where it had been. He sat on the top of the box for a couple of seconds, his nose and whiskers twitching.

"It looks as if he can still balance all right," said James.

"He's wobbling a little," said Mandy, "but not much!" Then she smiled as Harvey jumped down and ran to the other end of the boat to the maze she'd made with the small boxes.

*He's going to the one where I've hidden the cheese!*
thought Mandy, watching with big, round eyes.

Harvey carried the little square of cheese
out, jumped over the side of the boat, and put
the cheese down in the middle of his cage.
Then he climbed back onto the boat and into
the maze. This time he made straight for the
box with the sunflower seed.

Mandy and James listened carefully and then
grinned at each other. They could hear the
gerbil munching on it.

"I wonder if he'll find the carrot next," said Mandy.

Harvey went into the box with the carrot, but he came out quickly, jumped over the side again, and made his way to the piece of cheese. He ate about half of it, then sat on his haunches and rubbed his paws over his face. He was cleaning himself!

He cleaned his eyes, his ears, his nose, and his mouth, then he lowered his front legs to the ground and ran into his nesting box.

"Wow!" said James. "He had a really good time."

"I think he's starting to get quite tame already," said Mandy. "I'm sure he kept checking to see if we were watching when he was playing on his boat."

Mandy gave a small sigh as they went out of the unit. The quicker Harvey became tame, the quicker they'd have to try to find a home for him!

Mr. Jordan was in the waiting room with Arnie, so Mandy and James went to say hello.

"What's wrong with Arnie?" Mandy asked, bending to stroke him.

"He decided he wanted to look after the kitten next door," said Mr. Jordan. "He ran in through the cat flap, then got stuck!" Mr. Jordan didn't have a cat. But Mandy knew he lived in the house in Meadow Lane where the Greenes used to live. They'd probably put the cat flap in the door for their cat.

The cat's name was Tabby and she'd had six kittens just before the Greenes had moved. Mandy had found them all a home at Westmoor House, a retirement home about a mile away.

"I had to give Arnie a good hard tug to get him out," Mr. Jordan explained. "The poor boy yelped quite hard. I think he's only a bit bruised, but we're going on vacation tomorrow, so I'm getting him checked just to be sure."

While Mandy and James petted Arnie, Mr. Jordan asked how the gerbil was. He'd heard all about him from Mandy's grandpa.

"He's so smart!" said James. "You should have seen him playing on the boat we made for him. He's really clever, isn't he, Mandy?"

Mandy nodded and felt a little sad again. "We'll need to find him a home soon," she said, looking hopefully up at Mr. Jordan. It would be great if Harvey could stay in Welford. Then she and James would be able to visit him.

Mr. Jordan shook his head. "I couldn't chance having a gerbil," he said. "Arnie would want to pick him up and carry him around. And *we* know he wouldn't hurt him but . . ."

Mandy nodded. "But Harvey wouldn't know that," she agreed. "He'd be frightened."

"Don't worry, Mandy," said James, as he got ready to go. "Harvey's going to turn into a really fantastic pet. I'm sure we'll be able to find him a good home."

# 9

# *A Brilliant Idea*

By the time the weekend came, Mandy and James weren't feeling so confident about Harvey. True, he always seemed to be waiting for them when they hurried to see him after school. He looked at them when they talked to him and he let them stroke him through the cage bars. But he still ran and hid in a tube or in his nesting box whenever they put anything in the cage or when they gave him fresh food and water.

And although he played all sorts of games in, on, and around the boxes on the cargo boat, he didn't pay attention to the wooden ball or the brick. Grandpa had brought a tiny terra-cotta plant pot, but Harvey ignored that, too.

On Saturday morning, Harvey wouldn't even come to the front of the cage when Mandy called him. He poked his head out of his nesting box, but that was all.

"I don't think he's sick," she said to James. "He's eaten quite a lot of the food we gave him yesterday afternoon and his eyes are nice and bright."

"He just seems to have gone back to being nervous," sighed James. "Let's go away for a little while. He might be all right when we come back."

When they went back a couple of hours later, Harvey was standing up at the cage bars.

But he ran off when Mandy tried to stroke his tummy.

Mandy and James mentioned the problem to Simon, and he suggested Mandy make a play area for Harvey.

"Your hands might not seem so big and threatening inside a larger space," he said. "And he might play with more things if he had more room to play in. There are quite a few tall cardboard boxes waiting to be collected for recycling. You could use them as a barrier."

"We could put his cage inside the area and leave the door open," said Mandy. "And if Harvey comes out, we can take his cage away and clean it out. It's a great idea. Thanks, Simon!"

Dr. Emily said they could make a play area in the kitchen as long as they protected the floor with cardboard and paper. "And," she advised, "when you take his cage away, take the nesting box out of it and put it in the play area. Then Harvey will know he's got somewhere safe to run to."

While Mandy was getting the tall cardboard boxes, James went to get something from the saddlebag on his bike.

"Apple tree twigs and cotton string," he said to Mandy. "I thought we could try making a ladder."

Twenty minutes later, Harvey emerged cautiously through his cage door. He wiggled his nose and twitched his whiskers, then scurried toward the cargo boat. Mandy had put it on top of another box and James had put the twig ladder at the end where the maze was. On top of one of the tiny boxes was a special piece of gerbil chocolate.

In no time at all Harvey climbed up the ladder. Squeaking excitedly, he sniffed at the chocolate drop before eating it. Then he sat up on his haunches as if to say, "What's next?"

Mandy leaned over very slowly, lifted the cage out, and passed it to her friend. James removed the nesting box and carefully put it in the palms of his hands. Then he lowered it carefully into one corner of Harvey's play area.

"Keep your hands under it, James," said Mandy. "Harvey's watching, aren't you, boy?"

Harvey popped into the nesting box and then popped out again — scampering over James's fingers both times.

Mandy tiptoed to the kitchen table and got another piece of chocolate. Then she stuck it between two of James's fingertips. She didn't have time to move away before Harvey darted over to nibble at the chocolate treat. And when he'd finished it, he sniffed at Mandy's hand.

"I haven't got any," she told him. "How about a little stroke instead?"

Harvey didn't move, so Mandy stroked him under the chin with one finger. He stared solemnly up at her as she stroked him, talking softly all the time.

After a while, Harvey squeaked and moved away.

"He's sniffing at the wooden ball," said James. "He's . . . Oh, wow, Mandy!"

They stared in delight as Harvey pushed the ball with his nose, ran after it, and pushed it again. "He's playing soccer," said Mandy.

James leaned over one of the tall boxes and held his hands in a butterfly shape. "Nose the ball to me, Harvey," he said.

Harvey blinked. Then he nosed the ball hard and sent it straight into James's hands. "Goal!" breathed James.

"That was just luck," said Mandy. "He couldn't really have understood."

But James carefully rolled the ball back to the gerbil. "To me, Harvey," he said. And Harvey nosed it back.

"He's a genius!" said Mandy after Harvey had "scored" five goals. "A *gerbil genius!*"

She picked up the ball, made a cup shape with her hand, and rested it on the floor. Harvey scampered over and hopped into her hand. Mandy held her breath and wondered if she

dared to try putting her other hand over the top of Harvey's body.

"Go on," said James when she glanced at him.

"It's okay, Harvey," she murmured. "I won't squash you. What a brave boy." *She was holding Harvey. She was holding him at last!*

After a few seconds, Mandy raised her hands carefully, keeping them close to her body with Harvey facing toward her. And he didn't seem to mind at all!

"I think he likes it!" said James. He'd moved to stand as close as he could. "Look, he's put his face out. He's sniffing at your T-shirt."

Mandy lowered her face and rubbed her nose against Harvey's. And when Harvey looked at her with his big, dark, chocolate-brown eyes, Mandy felt happy and sad at the same time. Harvey was beginning to trust them at last. But now, they'd really have to start trying to find a home for him!

On Monday morning Mandy and James talked to some of their friends about Harvey. They were on their way down to the reed beds to do another mouse count.

There wouldn't be many more mouse counts after this. They knew now that there were harvest mice living near the reeds in Welford — and the reports from the other schools taking part in the survey showed which other areas were home to them as well.

"And even if Welford hasn't got the *most* harvest mice, our results will be the most unusual, because we found Harvey in one of our mouse houses!" said Mandy.

She and James had given a "Harvey update" after assembly, so everyone knew the gerbil was doing well. Since nobody had claimed him, he was now nearly ready to go to a new home.

"Gerbils are happier when they've got another gerbil to play with," said Mandy. "Like Terry and Gerry. But it says in one of my books that they should be introduced to each other before they're eight weeks old or they'll fight. My mom thinks Harvey's five or six months old."

"That means finding somewhere special for Harvey," James said. "He'll need a home where there's someone to play soccer with him and teach him more games. He's *so* smart, he loves learning things!"

When they reached the mouse houses, to Mandy's surprise, James didn't seem to be very interested in what they were doing.

"Are you all right?" she asked after a while.

James nodded. "Just thinking," he said. Then suddenly he stopped dead. "Listen!" he said.

"I've got a brilliant idea! I don't know *how* we didn't think of it before!"

Everyone else stopped whatever they were in the middle of doing with the tennis ball mouse houses and looked at James. They could tell he was excited.

"Wouldn't Mrs. Black's class be the perfect place for Harvey?" said James. "We don't have a class pet."

"Let's ask Mrs. Black about it right now!" said Amy Fenton.

"Yes!" said Paul. "It is a great idea, James!"

"No, don't ask yet!" Mandy said urgently. "When I was in Mrs. Black's class, I asked Mrs. Black if we could have a class pet."

"I remember that," said Pam Stanton. "She said she'd never have another class pet, because the last time she'd allowed her class to have a hamster she'd ended up looking after it herself."

Mandy nodded. "And she could never find anyone to take it home for the school vacations, so she had to do that, too!"

"Well, I couldn't have Harvey for the vacations because of Benji," James admitted gloomily. Benji was James's cat. "Maybe it wasn't such a good idea after all."

"It was, James," said Mandy. "There must be other kids who'd be able to take care of Harvey over the vacations."

"I'm sure I'd be able to," said Paul.

"I would, too," said Amy.

"So, we just need to think up a way of convincing Mrs. Black that there'd always be someone to look after Harvey at school and at home," said Mandy.

"She's coming over," whispered Amy. "Let's talk about it when we get back to school."

# 10

# *Making Plans*

Today, there were forty mouse houses without any seed left in them. Mrs. Todd and Mrs. Black couldn't understand why their pupils didn't seem more excited — or why they seemed so eager to get back to school!

Mandy and her friends *were* happy to know that even more harvest mice seemed to be using the special feeding houses, but making plans for Harvey to be Mrs. Black's class pet seemed much more important.

During lunch they all went into a little huddle in a corner of the playground.

Pam Stanton said she wished they had a photo of Harvey. "Then we could show it to Mrs. Black. She might think it was a shame that such a beautiful gerbil didn't have a home to go to," she said.

James looked at Paul. "You drew a great picture of Paddy," he said. "Could you come and see Harvey after school and draw a picture of him?"

Paul nodded. "You bet!" he said.

Mandy's eyes sparkled. "We could make the drawing into a card. A card with some rhymes inside . . ."

"Rhymes about a gerbil looking for a home," said Pam.

"A home where there are lots of children, somewhere he could learn things, because he loves learning!" said Amy.

"And we should have a rhyme about how well *we'd* look after him," said James.

"We can leave the card on Mrs. Black's desk with a bunch of flowers!" said Tina Cunningham. "I'm sure Dad will let me pick some out of the garden."

They spent the rest of recess coming up with rhymes. Mandy and James said they would write the card while Paul drew his picture of Harvey.

"And Mrs. Black always goes straight into the classroom when she arrives," said Mandy. "If we all get here a few minutes early tomorrow, we can put the flowers and the card on her desk."

"Then we can peep through the window and watch her face when she reads the card," said James.

Everything went according to plan next morning. Mandy and James had written the Harvey poem on the inside of a piece of folded paper and Paul had drawn Harvey on the outside. It was a really good drawing of Harvey standing up against the bars of his cage. Paul had drawn a speech bubble coming from the gerbil's mouth and inside it he'd written: *Please let me come to school and be your pet!*

Tina Cunningham had brought flowers wrapped in paper, tied with a bow, and Mr. Simpson, the janitor, had allowed James to go into the classroom early and put the card and the flowers on Mrs. Black's desk.

Now they were all looking in at the window, watching Mrs. Black.

"She's smiling," Mandy whispered.

"I bet that's at my line," said James. "It wasn't a very good one."

" *'This gerbil genius will be very happy to be with us . . . if we have him as our class pet. He'll behave very well and listen and learn . . . because that's what classrooms are for!'* " Mandy quoted with a giggle.

"Mine was worse than that!" Pam laughed. " *'Harvey the gerbil is feeling blue. Mrs. Black's got a heart of gold. If she'd allow Harvey to come to school, too, we'd look after him without being told!'* "

Just then, Paul gave a little gasp. Mrs. Black was coming over to the window.

"And what about school vacations?" she asked, popping her head out. "Who'll look after him then?"

Tina, Paul, and Amy dug into their backpacks and each pulled out a letter. "We thought of that, Mrs. Black!" said Amy. "These are from our parents saying we can take Harvey home for vacations."

"We can take turns," said Paul.

"What's he going to live in?" asked Mrs. Black.

They all looked at each other in dismay. They hadn't thought of that.

But then Mandy smiled. "I'm sure Mom and Dad would let us borrow a cage from Animal Ark for a while," she said.

"While we all save up our pocket money to buy him a cage of his own," said Paul. The others nodded.

"Very well," said Mrs. Black. "I'll have a word with Mrs. Garvie during morning break. *If* she agrees, I'll agree to a . . ." she held up a hand as everyone cheered, ". . . to a trial period," she said. "But if Harvey stops you from concentrating on your lessons, or if I think he isn't being well cared for . . ."

"We'll make a list like Mrs. Todd has for looking after Terry and Gerry," said James. "We'll all take turns to do the important things like feeding him and changing his water and cleaning the cage."

"And when you let us choose a reward for finishing our work early, we could choose to play with Harvey," said Tina.

The lining-up bell rang just then. They all sped away and got in line, standing straight and quiet! They were all silently wishing hard for Mrs. Garvie to say yes.

The first part of the morning seemed to go really slowly. And, for once, when recess came, everybody wanted it to end quickly!

Then they wanted it to last longer, because Mrs. Black came into the playground to tell them that Mrs. Garvie had agreed to let them have Harvey for a trial period of two weeks!

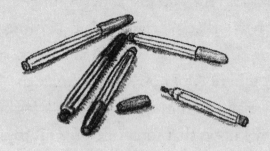

# 11

# *Harvey on Trial*

"You'll never guess what Harvey does now!" Mandy said excitedly to her mom and Simon one day after school.

It was almost two weeks since Dr. Emily had driven Mandy to school with Harvey in the cage that was on loan from Animal Ark. And every day Mandy came home and told her parents and Simon what the gerbil had been up to.

"Well, every time the bell for recess rings, he squeaks and runs up his ladder! Our class was in with Mrs. Black's class today, because we're making a huge map so we can mark off the places where we know harvest mice are living. And we all saw him do it. We think it's because Harvey knows that someone puts his toys in his cage when the bell rings, so he can have recess, too!"

"I expect he'd run up his ladder and squeak if he heard a whistle or some other noise," said Simon.

"Do you think so?" Mandy looked disappointed. "I'll ask Mrs. Black if we can try him with other noises tomorrow," she said.

When Mandy asked next day, Mrs. Black and Mandy's teacher, Mrs. Todd, thought the experiment was a good idea. They decided that the two classes should try it out just before morning recess.

The teachers had opened the dividing doors between the classrooms, because the two classes were working together again on the big map.

A short time before the bell for recess was due to ring, the classes stopped their lesson, and Mrs. Black gave a good, long blow on her playground whistle.

Harvey rose up onto his haunches and stood stock-still. Mrs. Black blew the whistle again — Harvey didn't move. Then Mrs. Todd said that might be because everyone was kneeling on the floor, watching him. "You all start to get up when the bell rings," she pointed out. "I'll make the alarm on my traveling clock buzz and you go to your tables and shuffle papers and push your chairs back."

The alarm clock buzzer sounded and everyone dashed to a table and pretended to be getting ready for break. But still Harvey didn't go to his ladder.

It was only when the real break bell sounded that Harvey dashed to his ladder and ran up it, squeaking louder than ever.

"It seems there's no fooling Harvey," said Mrs. Black, smiling. "He really is a gerbil genius!"

When the others went out to play, Amy Fenton and James stayed behind. Today was one of the days for cleaning out Harvey's cage. On those days, instead of going to the teacher's room, Mrs. Black stayed in the classroom during morning recess with whoever was cleaning out Harvey's cage.

James went to get the big cardboard box with tall sides that they put Harvey into while his cage was being cleaned, and Amy lifted the gerbil out. She was careful to hold him facing her body so he couldn't suddenly jump and land on the floor.

Harvey sat in her hand, twitching his nose as she talked to him. But the second James came and put the box on the floor, he gave a loud squeak.

"He's being clever again," laughed Amy as she lowered Harvey into the box. "He *knows* there are lots of playthings in here."

"He'll start looking for his wooden ball in a minute," said James, as he went to the cage and started to remove the soiled wood chips from the bottom of it.

"I've hidden it under one of the small boxes," he added, glancing across at Mrs. Black. "Harvey will sniff at all the boxes until he finds the right one. Then he'll lift it up with his nose and push it out of the way so he can get the ball."

"That's amazing!" laughed Mrs. Black when Harvey did exactly as James had said he would.

Then she turned as someone knocked on the classroom door. "That should be Mrs. Garvie with my cup of coffee," she said.

"Did you hear that, Harvey?" Amy whispered as Mrs. Black went to open the door. "Mrs. Black said you were amazing! I'm sure she's going to let you stay."

"I heard that, Amy Fenton!" Mrs. Black walked back over with her drink. Amy turned pink and her teacher smiled. "But I must admit you're all taking very good care of him," she said.

"And of his cage," she added, as James went to the sink to scrub Harvey's food dish and water container.

A few minutes later, they heard the lining-up bell. "Gosh!" said James. "I haven't finished Harvey's cage yet." He threw a worried look toward Mrs. Black.

"It's all right, James," she said. "Break started late because of our experiment. I'll give you a few minutes at lunchtime to finish."

"Will he mind going into his cage when

there aren't any wood chips on the floor?" Amy asked anxiously.

"Leave him in his box," said Mrs. Black. "But," she warned as the others came in from the playground, "there'll be big trouble if anyone so much as looks toward the box. I want us to get all the areas marked out on the map this morning."

"I think Mrs. Black might be carrying out a little experiment of her own," James whispered when Mrs. Black was at the far end of the room, handing out colored pens.

Amy nodded. "Seeing if we can behave when we know Harvey isn't in his cage."

It was so interesting finding the areas where all the other schools had carried out their surveys and then drawing tiny pictures of tennis ball mouse houses that nobody looked up from the map at all.

"You're all doing really well," said Mrs. Todd, kneeling down next to Mandy.

"I think we've just about finished," said

Mandy. "We've written the names of the schools as well as drawing mouse houses in the places each school put them. We can't write in how many harvest mice there are in each area until Mrs. Garvie gets the last reports."

"But we can write in how many we think there are in Welford," said James. "We had our last mouse counting day last week."

Mandy gasped and looked at Mrs. Todd. "We haven't marked our school or the reed beds on the map!" she said.

"I wondered when you'd realize that," her teacher smiled.

"So," said Mrs. Black, from where she was kneeling at the other side of the map. "Who's going to be the first to find Welford?"

Everyone knelt closer over the big map. But suddenly, there was a funny little scuffling noise, and James jumped as he felt something brush past his leg and against the inside of his arm.

"Harvey!" he said in astonishment as the gerbil scampered onto the map. "Quick, everyone! Move closer together so he can't escape!"

But Harvey didn't make any attempt to move off the map. Nose down, he ran back and forth and from side to side over it. Then suddenly he stopped. He rose up onto his haunches and stared around at everyone in turn, his brown eyes shining brightly.

"Well," Mrs. Black said softly. "I think that settles it, doesn't it?"

"It's the first time he's disturbed us during a lesson, Mrs. Black," pleaded Amy. "Please give him another chance."

"He must have managed to climb up the side of the box," said James. "If you'll give him another chance, we promise we'll never leave him in it again, unless we're watching him!"

"And — " began Mandy. But she stopped when Mrs. Black held up a hand for silence.

"You can't imagine that I wouldn't let Harvey stay after this!" she said. "Just look at him. Look at *where* he's sitting!"

"Oh!" said James, his eyes huge and round behind his glasses. "He's . . . he's sitting on Welford!" he stuttered.

"That's right," Mrs. Black smiled.

"More than that," said Mrs. Todd. "He's sitting exactly on top of where we want to mark Welford Village School."

Mrs. Black nodded and leaned forward to pick up Harvey. "You're a gerbil genius," she told him. "We couldn't possibly let you go anywhere else now. You've shown us that Welford Village School is where you belong!"

Everyone cheered as Mrs. Black stood up and carried Harvey toward his cage.

"James! Amy!" she said over the cheers. "What are you waiting for? Come here and make Harvey's cage ready for him."

"Yes, Mrs. Black," laughed James and Amy as they leaped to their feet and hurried to do just that.

coming soon

# DUCKLING DIARY

by Ben M. Baglio

It was almost six weeks ago that she and James first spotted the duck building her nest. Two weeks to build it . . . four weeks to sit on the eggs. She looked at the dates, carefully written down since that first day. Her heart pounded with excitement as she worked the dates out.

She ran downstairs to the phone and quickly dialed James's number.

"James," she said before he'd even had a chance to say hello. "The eggs. They're due to hatch tomorrow!"

"Tomorrow!" James said. "That's great!"

"Come over as early as you can," Mandy said.

"I will," James said. "Definitely."

The following morning, Mandy was up bright and early. The warm mist promised another fine spring day. She waited eagerly at the gate for James and soon spotted him rushing down the street. Blackie was bounding ahead of James.

"Won't it be great if the eggs really do hatch today?" James's voice was full of excitement.

"Yes!" Mandy said. "My book said incubation varies from twenty-eight to thirty days. Today's the twenty-eighth day, I'm sure. So let's keep our fingers crossed."

118

When they approached the pond, they suddenly heard a terrible, frantic quacking and a splashing of water. Then a beating of wings. They saw a duck fly up and away toward the cornfield, shrieking in terror.

Mandy looked at James in horror. "That's our duck!" she cried. "Quick!"

They ran as fast as they could through the long grass toward the pond.

At the water's edge, a terrible scene met their eyes. Mandy's hand flew to her mouth, and she stood there in stunned silence.

"Oh, no!" James exclaimed in a horrified voice.

The little bankside island was empty. It *was* the mother duck they had seen. Her nest had been destroyed, and she had flown away. There was no sign of the eggs. All that was left were reeds and twigs floating around the island in sad little bundles.

"Poor duck!" Mandy wailed. "What will she do now?" Tears rolled down her cheeks.

Blackie came and licked her hand. He always seemed to know when people were upset.

James was almost crying, too. "Who could have done it?" he asked, shaking his head.

Suddenly, Blackie bounded off toward the little island. There didn't seem to be much point in going after him. The duck had been frightened away already. Blackie sniffed around in the long grass for a minute and then came trotting back.

Mandy was still sobbing.

"I bet it was a fox," James said.

"Yes," Mandy agreed tearfully. "I know foxes have to eat, but why did a fox have to attack *our* duck?"

Blackie placed something on the grass in front of Mandy. Then he nudged her knee. It was an egg. A duck egg. A perfect, unbroken duck egg.

Forgetting her tears, Mandy picked it up and cradled it gently in her hands. It was still warm! "Oh, James," she whispered.

James stared at the egg and gave Blackie a big hug. "Good boy, Blackie!"

"James," Mandy said urgently. "Do you remember when Libby Masters's pet hen, Rhonda, was hatching her chicks? Rhonda could only leave the eggs for a few minutes, otherwise they would get cold, and the chicks inside would die."

James nodded. "Yes," he said. "We've got to keep this egg warm and get it somewhere it can stay warm as fast as we can, so the baby duck inside doesn't die."

"Grandma and Grandpa are closest," Mandy said.

"Right," James replied. "Come on!"

With Mandy holding the egg in both hands close to her body for warmth, they hurried toward Lilac Cottage.

Grandpa was surprised to see the three of them so early in the day, although he had been up for a long time. He was in his greenhouse tying up a web of string to support his budding tomato plants. Grandma had just gone out shopping.

"What on earth's wrong?" Grandpa asked when he saw their anxious faces.

"Oh, Grandpa!" Mandy quickly told him what had happened. "Where can we put the egg to keep it warm?"

"The linen closet should do for the time being," Grandpa replied.

They all hurried indoors. Mandy walked carefully up the stairs and placed the egg on a bundle of Grandma's snowy white towels on the shelf nearest the hot water tank.

"That should do it," she murmured. She touched the shell gently with her fingertip. "Now you keep nice and warm, baby duck. We're going to look after you, so you needn't worry." She closed the linen closet door softly and ran back downstairs.

Grandpa and James were sitting at the kitchen table.

"Well," Grandpa said. "Now what are you going to do?"